W9-CBH-325

THE CHRISTMAS

EVE TREE

For Ben and Sydell
E.S.

Text copyright © 2015 by the Estate of Delia Huddy
Illustrations copyright © 2015 by Emily Sutton

First U.S. edition 2016

Library of Congress Catalog Card Number 2015940365
ISBN 978-0-7636-7917-0

16 17 18 19 20 21 CCP 10 9 8 7 6 5 4 3 2 1

Printed in Shenzhen, Guangdong, China

This book was typeset in Clarendon T Light.
The illustrations were done in watercolor.

Candlewick Press
99 Dover Street
Somerville, Massachusetts 02144

visit us at www.candlewick.com

THE CHRISTMAS EVE TREE

Delia Huddy

illustrated by EMILY SUTTON

CANDLEWICK PRESS

A
forest of
Christmas trees
stretching over the hills.
That's where the story begins.
There the little fir tree was planted,
but planted carelessly,
so that when the wind blew strong
it fell sideways onto its neighbor
and had no chance to grow.

The years went by until one December, when the foresters dug up trees for the Christmas market, the little fir tree, stunted and still tangled with its neighbor, was loaded onto a trailer and driven down the highway to the city.

"Oh, my," it said breathlessly,
for it was at the bottom of the pile.

The tallest trees were unroped
and taken away:

one to stand
proudly in a cathedral,

another in the middle
of a large square,

and a third to decorate the stage at a grand Christmas ball.

But most of the trees were bought by ordinary folks, for houses where there were children who covered them with stars and red tinsel, chocolate mice and small secret packages.

The little fir tree and its companion were taken to a large store,

where late on Christmas Eve they were the only trees still

unsold. A shopper hurried in to make a last-minute purchase.

"You won't want this scraggly thing, miss,"

said the store clerk as he pulled the little fir tree

from the branches of the bigger tree and tossed it aside.

The customer smiled and went off, pleased with her find.

But the little fir tree worried about what its fate might be.

There was a boy in the shop,

drawn in from the cold outside by the warmth

and the lights and the wonderful spicy smell of Christmas.

He said, "You throwing that away? Could I have it?"

The clerk looked at the little fir tree—

hardly what you'd call a tree at all. He shrugged

and handed it over. After all, it was Christmas Eve

and the store would soon be closing.

The boy went outside into the cheerless evening. He held
the little fir tree carefully in front of him so that none
of its few crooked branches would get snapped off by
shoppers on the sidewalk. He set off on the long walk
to the river. On his way, he found a cardboard box
in a trash can and brought it along, too.

When he came to the shore,
the tide was out, and down the steps
a small pebbly beach was showing.
The boy climbed down and,
digging the mud with his hands,
planted the little fir tree
in the cardboard box.

Near the steps, under the arches of a railway bridge,

the boy had another cardboard box, big enough to sleep in.

He put the tree on the pavement in front of him.

What a poor thing I am, thought the little fir tree,

but the boy seemed pleased, so the little fir tree felt more cheerful.

I belong to someone now, it thought to itself.

And it began to feel like Christmas.

A passerby dropped a coin in the boy's lap.

It was enough to buy him dinner,

but instead he crossed over to the newsstand

and bought some candles and a box of matches.

He attached the candles to the branches

of the little fir tree.

Now other people were returning

to claim their cardboard boxes for the night.

They gathered around the boy and the little fir tree.

An old street performer with an accordion sat down,

and soon the notes of a Christmas song

blended with the heavy rumble of the trains overhead.

Everyone started to sing.

More people gathered: homebound travelers, theatergoers,
sightseers. A policeman tried to move them on,
but they stood where they were, singing,
and the traffic was brought to a halt.

The candles burned steadily

and the old man played, and still the people sang.

The little fir tree felt it would burst with happiness,

because clearly the boy had forgotten

that tonight he would be sleeping in a cardboard box

under the railway arch, and that tomorrow

he would eat not turkey but soup in a soup kitchen,

if he was lucky.

A few days later the boy moved on.

"You're more dead than alive," he said sadly

to the little fir tree as he went.

And the tree, feeling dry and brittle, had to agree.

But while other Christmas trees

were piled onto January bonfires, the little fir tree

was put in a street sweeper's wheelbarrow.

"There's a green shoot here," said the street sweeper,
looking at the tree's roots, and slyly he planted it
in the corner of a park.

There you will find it. Not so little now,

for against all odds it grew—if not big and tall,

at least cheerfully stout.

Now it stretches out its branches for sparrows, pigeons,
babies in strollers, lovers, and office workers.
Mice nibble at its roots.

And as the winter days shorten,

the fir tree dreams of its poor beginnings

in the hills . . . of that magical Christmas Eve . . .

and of sunny days in the park.

Who would have thought? it says to itself

as it looks forward to another spring.

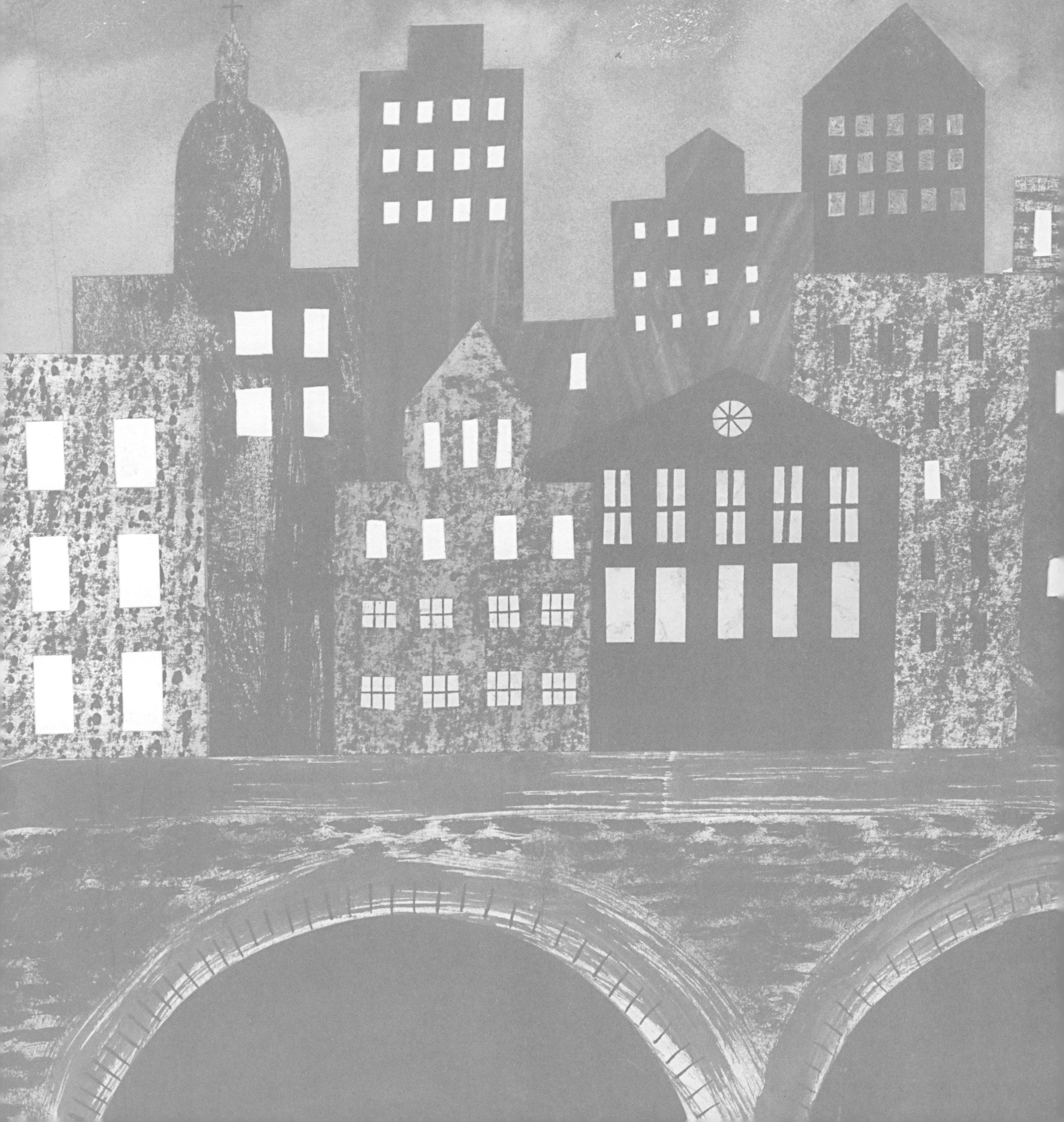